POLLY'S PUFFIN

Sarah Garland

The Bodley Head
London

Polly did not like shopping with Baby Jim.

He never stopped throwing things.

One day, when they stopped to have a cup of tea,

Polly let Jim play with her puffin,
for a treat.

This was a big mistake.

First Jim hugged it.

Then he kissed it.

Then, with all his might and main
he threw it...

straight into the hood
of a duffle-coated gentleman.

Never noticing the puffin, the man walked quickly through the door.

Polly leapt to her feet.

They ran through the fashion department.

They went up the escalator – but the man was going down.

They left the shop just in time to see…

the man turning a corner.

They followed him
into a church.

Up the tower
they climbed,
higher and
higher,

until they reached the top.
But the man was nowhere
to be seen.

And when they reached the street again
he had completely disappeared.

They searched the market.

They asked at the library.

They hunted through the pet shop.

At last they turned for home.

Polly thought she would never
see her puffin again.

But she was wrong!

And the next time they went shopping,
Polly thought she might leave her
puffin safely at home.